Vera Rides a Bike

Vera Rosenberry

Henry Holt and Company

New York

Henry Holt and Company, LLC
Publishers since 1866
115 West 18th Street
New York, New York 10011
www.henryholt.com

Henry Holt is a registered trademark of Henry Holt and Company, LLC
Distributed in Canada by H. B. Fenn and Company Ltd.

Library of Congress Cataloging-in-Publication Data
Rosenberry, Vera.
Vera rides a bike / Vera Rosenberry.
Summary: Vera learns to ride her new bicycle, but she has a little trouble stopping.
[1. Bicycles and bicycling—Fiction.] I. Title.
PZ7.R719155Vcf 2004   [E]—dc21   2003007068

ISBN 0-8050-7125-3 / First Edition—2004
Printed in the United States of America on acid-free paper. ∞

1 3 5 7 9 10 8 6 4 2

The artist used watercolor on Lanaquarelle paper to create the illustrations for this book.

For Raman. This is really his story — and in memory of his beautiful red tricycle.

One fragrant spring day,
Vera and her mother went to the park.

Vera rode her tricycle. She whistled a cheery tune
as she pushed the pedals up and down.

Vera loved her bright red tricycle. There was a round bell on the right handlebar, and streamers flowed out of the hand grips. Crepe paper from the Fourth of July parade was still threaded around the front wheel.

Inside the park, Vera and her mother watched some fish swimming in a fountain. The sun warmed Vera's face and made golden patterns in the cold water as she dipped her hands in and out, hoping a fish would swish against them.

Vera and her mother turned back to continue along the path. But Vera's
tricycle was no longer where she had left it.

"MY TRICYCLE!" Vera cried, suddenly feeling dizzy and sick.

Vera stared at the empty spot. No one was in sight, and it was so quiet
even the birds had stopped singing. Dark clouds bubbled up in the sky.

Vera and her mother looked
everywhere for her tricycle.

They reported its disappearance to the park
police officer, who took notes in a tiny book.

It began to rain. Sadly, Vera
and her mother walked home.
   "Maybe someone will find it,"
Mother said as she squeezed
Vera's hand. But no one did.

Weeks went by, and summer came. Vera missed her tricycle. She moped on the front steps.

"You were too big for it anyway," said her sister Elaine. "Your knees bumped the handlebars."

"I know," Vera replied. "But it was my very own tricycle, and I loved it."

Sometimes Elaine would let Vera practice balancing
on her big blue bicycle. Vera sat on the crossbar and scraped
her feet along the ground, then raised them up to coast.
But Elaine's bike was too big for Vera to ride properly.

One Saturday, Vera's father said he had a surprise.
There, in the driveway, was a small green bicycle,
just the right size for Vera.

"This was Elaine's first bicycle," her father said.
"I repaired it and painted it your favorite color.
It was supposed to be for your birthday in
November, but since your tricycle is gone, you
may have it now."

Vera remembered the broken
and battered little bike, which
used to be purple. She liked it
much better green, and it looked
new again. She kicked up the stand
and happily walked her beautiful bicycle
down the driveway.

"Here," said her mother. "You will need this."

Vera carefully strapped on a new white helmet.

Father held the bike, and she mounted the seat.

Her feet reached the pedals perfectly. Vera felt very big.

"Maybe we ought to put on training wheels,"
Father suggested.

"No, thank you," said Vera. "I don't need
them. I can balance well already."

Father ran along the sidewalk, holding the bicycle while
Vera learned to pedal. After a while, he occasionally let go.

Almost every day after dinner, Father or Mother helped Vera ride her bicycle in the school yard. Soon she could balance by herself after someone started her off. Then she would circle around and call out when she needed to be stopped.

One evening, everyone was busy when Vera
wanted to ride her bike. She put on her helmet
and walked her bike to the school yard alone.

Vera saw Norman. He was going down the slide headfirst.

"I bet you can't ride that bike by yourself," Norman said.

"Yes, I can," Vera replied. "But will you hold it so I can start?"

"Sure," Norman agreed.

Vera proudly rode around the school on
the smooth slate sidewalk. Norman was now
on the swing set, watching her. He waved
as she flew by.

After a long time, Vera wanted to stop. She looked for Norman.
He was not on the swing set anymore. Vera rode around again.

"Norman!" she called, pedaling slowly.

Norman was not in the sandbox. He was not on the slide or the
monkey bars. He must have gone home. Around and around Vera
went. She wanted to go home, too.

"HELP!" Vera yelled.
"I CAN'T STOP!"

But there was no one in the school yard to hear her. The sun was beginning to set. Vera thought maybe she could ride all the way home, but she would have to cross some streets, and she couldn't stop to look for cars.

Around and around and around Vera went. Her legs were tired, and the air was chilly.

Finally, Vera said firmly, "I will just have to use the brakes and stop myself, or I will be here all night."

Vera turned into the big kite-flying field to help her slow down. She closed her eyes tight and pressed backward very hard on the pedals. Her bicycle stopped, but Vera didn't— she flew into the air and onto the long, soft grass.

Vera lay in the sweet-smelling field.
It was quiet, and she was happy to be
still at last. Carefully, she got up and
dusted herself off.

Her knees and elbows were
skinned and grass stained, but
she was not hurt.

By now, the sky was almost dark. Vera walked her bicycle home as quickly as she could. She shivered, and her legs felt rubbery.

In front of her house, Vera's parents ran up to meet her.

"Where have you been, Vera?" they asked. "It is nearly dark. We were so worried!" But when they saw how tired and dirty Vera looked, they were just happy she was safely home.

Vera's legs and arms were not working very well.
Mother had to help her take a bath.

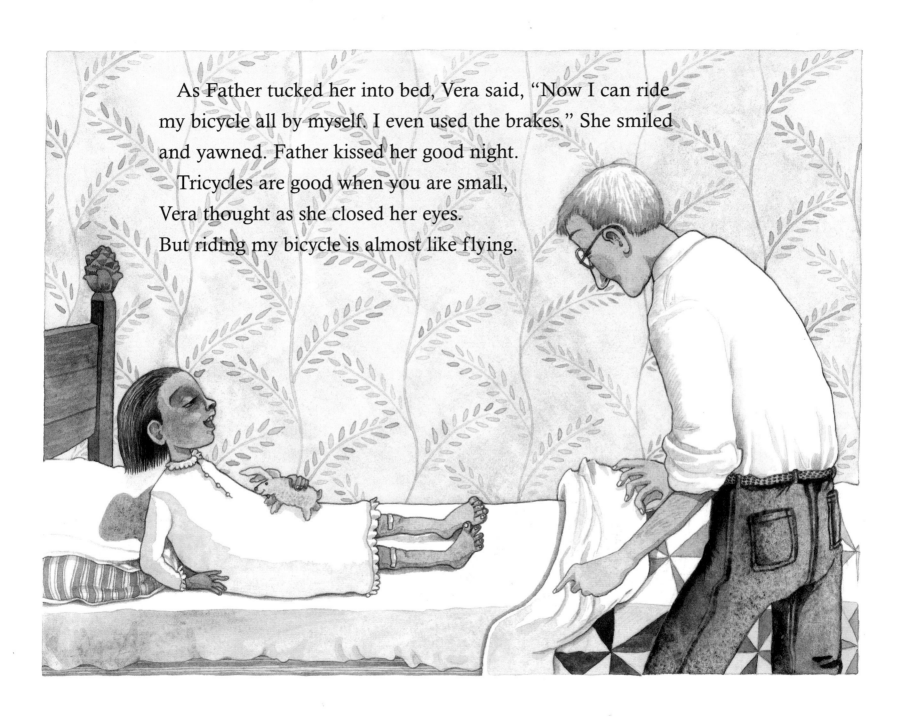

As Father tucked her into bed, Vera said, "Now I can ride
my bicycle all by myself. I even used the brakes." She smiled
and yawned. Father kissed her good night.

Tricycles are good when you are small,
Vera thought as she closed her eyes.
But riding my bicycle is almost like flying.